Now You See Them, Now You Don't!

The kids were gathered around a campfire, roasting marshmallows, when Ron said, "Why doesn't Annie tell one of her famous ghost stories?"

"Okay," Annie said. "I'll tell you the story of the drinking horse of Galloping Grits."

Everyone became silent. The only sound was the crackle of the campfire.

Annie's eyes were on Nancy as she began to speak. "Every summer one pony on this ranch . . . disappears."

"Oh, no!" Bess gasped.

Annie nodded. And it always happens on the night of a full moon."

"There's a full moon tonight!" George declared. "I believe that story. Do you, Nancy?"

Nancy shook her head. "It's a good story. But ponies can't just disappear."

Bess gave a little shiver. "I sure hope not. . ." she said softly.

The Nancy Drew Notebooks

# 1	The Slumber Party Secret	#25	Dare at the Fair
# 2	The Lost Locket	#26	The Lucky Horseshoes
# 3	The Secret Santa	#27	Trouble Takes the Cake
# 4	Bad Day for Ballet	#28	Thrill on the Hill
# 5	The Soccer Shoe Clue	#29	Lights! Camera! Clues!
# 6	The Ice Cream Scoop	#30	It's No Joke!
# 7	Trouble at Camp Treehouse	#31	The Fine Feathered Mystery
# 8	The Best Detective	#32	The Black Velvet Mystery
# 9	The Thanksgiving Surprise	#33	The Gumdrop Ghost
#10	Not Nice on Ice	#34	Trash or Treasure?
#11	The Pen Pal Puzzle	#35	Third-Grade Reporter
#12	The Puppy Problem	#36	The Make-Believe Mystery
#13	The Wedding Gift Goof	#37	Dude Ranch Detective
#14	The Funny Face Fight	#38	Candy Is Dandy
#15	The Crazy Key Clue	#39	The Chinese New Year Mystery
#16	The Ski Slope Mystery	#40	Dinosaur Alert!
#17	Whose Pet Is Best?	#41	Flower Power
#18	The Stolen Unicorn	#42	Circus Act
#19	The Lemonade Raid	#43	The Walkie-Talkie Mystery
#20	Hannah's Secret	#44	The Purple Fingerprint
#21	Princess on Parade	#45	The Dashing Dog Mystery
#22	The Clue in the Glue	#46	The Snow Queen's Surprise
#23	Alien in the Classroom		
#24	The Hidden Treasures		

THE NANCY DREW NOTEBOOKS®

#37

Dude Ranch Detective

CAROLYN KEENE
ILLUSTRATED BY JAN NAIMO JONES

Aladdin Paperbacks
New York   London   Toronto   Sydney   Singapore

This book is a work of fiction. Any references to historical events, real people, or real locales are used fictitiously. Other names, characters, places, and incidents are the product of the author's imagination, and any resemblance to actual events or locales or persons, living or dead, is entirely coincidental.

First Aladdin Paperbacks edition May 2002
First Minstrel Books edition August 2000

Copyright © 2000 by Simon & Schuster, Inc.

ALADDIN PAPERBACKS
An imprint of Simon & Schuster
Children's Publishing Division
1230 Avenue of the Americas
New York, NY 10020

The text of this book was set in Excelsior.

Printed in the United States of America
10 9 8 7 6 5 4

NANCY DREW and THE NANCY DREW NOTEBOOKS
are registered trademarks of Simon & Schuster, Inc.

ISBN 0-671-04268-8

Dude Ranch Detective

1

Ride 'Em, Cowgirls!

Are these cowboy hats for us, Slim?" eight-year-old Nancy Drew asked the tall man in the gift shop.

"You bet," Slim said. He tipped his own white cowboy hat. "Compliments of the Galloping Grits Dude Ranch."

"Cool!" Nancy's best friend George Fayne said. She placed the cowboy hat over her dark curls. "Now we're real cowboys!"

"Cow-*girls*," Bess Marvin said. Bess was Nancy's other best friend. She was also George's cousin. "Do these hats come in pink?" Bess asked Slim.

"A pink cowboy hat?" George cried. She rolled her eyes. "Give me a break!"

While Slim helped another customer, Nancy smiled. She couldn't believe she was on a ranch with real horses. Now she, Bess, and George could practice everything they had learned at the River Heights Riding Academy.

"This is going to be the best vacation ever," Nancy said. She gave Bess a hug. "It was nice of your parents to invite me and George to come along."

"It was Mom and Dad's idea," Bess said. She nodded at her parents, who were checking out postcards at the other side of the store. "They said there'd be plenty of room in our minivan."

"Yeah," George joked. "Even with all of Bess's suitcases."

"It's good to pack a lot of clothes," Bess insisted. "In case you need them."

"Like your ballet tutu?" George asked. "When are you going to need *that* on a dude ranch?"

Nancy saw Bess pout.

"It's okay, Bess," Nancy said. "I packed

2

a lot of things, too. Like my riding clothes, sneakers, bathing suits—"

"And your blue detective notebook, of course," Bess interrupted with a smile.

"Of course," Nancy said. "But this week I'm a detective *and* a cowgirl."

"I heard that," Slim said. His blue eyes twinkled as he walked back to the girls. "And you're not real cowgirls yet."

"We're not?" Bess asked.

"Nope," Slim said. "First you have to wave your hats in the air and shout—Yee-haaaa!"

The girls looked at one another. Then they took off their hats and waved them in the air. "Yee-haaaa!" they shouted.

"*Now* you're official cowboys," Slim said. "Whoops—I mean cowgirls!"

Nancy smiled at Slim. "Are you the owner of this ranch?" she asked.

"No," Slim said. "My wife, Dixie, and I are the head ranch hands. We're minding the ranch while the owners are away. And this gift shop, of course."

The girls began exploring the shop.

George picked up a T-shirt that read Horsing Around at Galloping Grits.

Nancy and Bess ran to a shelf filled with colorful wooden animals.

"I carve and paint those little critters myself," Slim told the girls.

Bess held up the bright blue wooden horse. She turned to her parents. "Mom, Dad? Can I have it? Please?"

Mrs. Marvin looked up from a postcard she was holding. "It's very nice, Bess," she said. "But we came to the ranch to see *real* horses, remember?"

Real horses! The words made Nancy shiver with excitement.

After buying the postcards, Mr. and Mrs. Marvin went to their cabin to unpack.

The girls got permission to explore the ranch. There were lots of kids running in and out of cabins and heading toward the lake with rubber rafts.

"Where are the animals?" Bess asked.

Nancy glanced around. She saw a big red barn with bales of hay piled up on one side. A row of log cabins stood

4

against the lake. There was a playground, a dining hall, and a tennis court next to the main house.

Then Nancy saw something black and white in the distance. It was standing on four legs.

"I think I see a cow," Nancy said.

"Let's *mooove* closer," George joked.

But as they got nearer Nancy noticed something strange about the cow.

"That cow's not real," Nancy said. She tilted her head. "It's a fake."

WHOOOOOOSH!

A white rope fell over Nancy's shoulder. It slipped down to her waist.

"Hey!" Nancy shouted. The rope dropped in a circle around her feet. She whirled around and saw a boy with blond hair and glasses wearing a cowboy hat.

"Can I have my lasso back?" the boy asked. He held the other end of the rope.

"What's the big idea?" George demanded.

"I was trying to rope Sylvia," the boy said. He pointed to the fake cow. "That's what she's here for—lasso practice."

Nancy stepped out of the rope. "Who are you?" she asked the boy.

The boy tipped his cowboy hat. "The name's Josh Fleckner," he said. "But you can call me Tex."

"Are you from Texas?" Bess asked.

"No. Chicago," Josh said. He pointed to a long white trailer next to the cabins. "My parents and I are driving all over the country this summer. The Galloping Grits Dude Ranch is the best part. Especially for a cowboy like me."

"What makes you a real cowboy?" George asked.

"Because I'm going to get my own pony, that's why," Josh said. "My mom and dad are bringing one back from the ranch."

"Wow!" Nancy said. "I hope your house has a very big yard."

"We live in an apartment." Josh shrugged. "But my room is big enough for a horse—if I move my bed against the wall."

Josh tipped his hat. He whistled as he walked away.

"What a pest," Bess whispered.

"The biggest pest in the West!" George giggled.

"Howdy, girls!" a voice called.

Nancy spun around. She saw a woman dressed in blue overalls walking over.

"I'm Slim's wife, Dixie," the woman explained. "It looks like you girls are enjoying your first day on the ranch."

"We are," Nancy said. "But there's one thing we can't wait to see."

"Hmm," Dixie said with a grin. "Let me guess. Could that be . . . the ponies?"

The girls jumped up and down.

"We took riding lessons!" Bess said excitedly. "We can even ride fast!"

"Well, now!" Dixie laughed. "How would you all like to come to the stable for your first trot around the corral?"

Nancy glanced at Bess and George. They looked just as excited as she was.

"We'd *love* it!" George exclaimed.

The girls followed Dixie to the stable. Nancy was glad they were already wearing their riding clothes.

When they entered the stable Nancy

saw eight stalls filled with ponies. Two teenagers were feeding them carrots.

"Meet our wranglers, Ron and Linda," Dixie said. "They work here every summer."

Ron and Linda smiled and nodded.

"I like that pony best," Bess said. She ran over to a white pony with a brown mane. "Which one do you like, Nancy?"

Nancy couldn't decide. Then she saw a black pony with a white star-shaped mark on his nose. His tail was black with silver streaks.

"He's beautiful!" Nancy gasped.

"Star is also worth a lot of money," Dixie said. She patted his mane. "You'll see why as soon as you ride him."

Nancy's eyes lit up. She was going to ride Star!

Bess chose the white pony named Peppermint. George picked Tawny, a tan pony with white speckles. Then Dixie, Ron, and Linda saddled the ponies and led them outside to the corral.

Nancy, Bess, and George waited outside the fence. A girl was already riding a pony. Her red hair flew back as she galloped around the corral.

"Look at her go!" George whistled.

"That's Annie, our junior wrangler," Dixie called out. "She's ten years old, and she's been riding since she was five."

When the ponies were lined up inside the corral Ron and Linda helped the girls mount. Nancy remembered what to do: step into the stirrup with the left foot and swing the right leg over the saddle. Soon all three friends were sitting in their saddles.

Annie slowed her pony down. She trotted over. "Dixie?" she asked. "Why is that girl riding Star?"

"It's okay, honey," Dixie said. "I just want to see how Nancy rides."

"Okay," Annie said over her shoulder as she rode her pony out of the corral. "But just today."

"Why doesn't Annie want me to ride Star?" Nancy asked Dixie.

"Star is Annie's favorite horse," Dixie replied. She rubbed her hands together.

"Now, why don't you girls show me what you learned in riding school?"

Nancy went first. She pulled gently on Star's reins. Then she pressed her legs against Star's sides and guided him toward the center of the corral.

Star snorted and began to trot. But it was more than just a trot—Star was prancing like a parade horse!

2

Annie's Story

Did you learn something in riding school that we didn't, Nancy?" Bess called from Peppermint.

"No!" Nancy said. She couldn't stop grinning. "Star is doing all the work!"

Star threw back his head and strutted around the corral.

"Way to go, Star!" George cheered.

Star stopped and straightened out one leg. Nancy held on tightly as he took a bow.

Just like a show horse, Nancy thought. She could see Annie leaning on the fence. Annie was watching Star, too.

12

All three girls rode their ponies around the corral. But Nancy knew that Star was special.

"You should change his name," Nancy told Annie as she rode over to the fence.

"To what?" Annie asked.

"Superstar!" Nancy declared.

Annie smiled. She climbed over the fence and grabbed Star's reins. "I think Star needs to rest now."

Already? Nancy thought. She swung her right leg over Star's back and dismounted.

"Can I ride Star tomorrow, Annie?" Nancy asked. "And the day after that?"

"We'll see," Annie said as she led Star back to the stable.

"'Bye, Star," Nancy whispered.

"You girls did great," Dixie said. "You can join the trail ride tomorrow morning at nine-thirty if you'd like."

"We'd like that very much!" Bess exclaimed.

Bess and George dismounted their ponies. Then Ron and Linda led Peppermint and Tawny back to the stable.

"I wish Annie had let me ride Star a little longer," Nancy said.

"Maybe Star was hot," Bess suggested.

George fanned herself with her cowboy hat. "He's not the only one. Let's ask if we can go swimming."

The girls ran to their cabin. After they had changed into their bathing suits, Mr. and Mrs. Marvin took them down to the lake.

Nancy, Bess, and George swam and splashed one another in the cool water. They made two new friends: nine-year-old Iris Park from Minnesota and eight-year-old Peter Sanchez from Philadelphia.

Bess and George stayed in the water, but Nancy dried herself off. She sat down at a picnic table and took out a postcard that Mrs. Marvin had given her.

I'm going to write to Daddy and Hannah, Nancy thought.

Hannah had been the Drews' housekeeper since Nancy was three years old.

Using her pencil with the blue dolphin eraser, Nancy began to write:

14

Dear Daddy and Hannah,

It's only our first day and I'm already having a great time. No mysteries yet, but that's okay. There are lots of other fun things to do here!

Love and XXX,
Nancy

"Don't eat the red-hot chili, girls," Mr. Marvin warned at the cookout that evening. "It's probably very spicy."

"You're eating it," George said to her uncle, pointing to his paper plate.

Mr. Marvin patted his stomach. "Nothing is too hot for these guts of steel," he said with a chuckle.

Nancy, Bess, and George watched as Mr. Marvin ate a forkful of chili. After a few seconds his face turned bright red.

"Water!" Mr. Marvin gasped. He grabbed a plastic pitcher and poured himself a big cup of water.

"I think I'll stick to the hot dogs," George whispered to Nancy and Bess.

After the cookout there was a campfire and a marshmallow roast for the kids. Iris and Peter were there. So was Annie. But when Nancy saw Josh she had to giggle. He was wearing a white cowboy outfit studded with red rhinestones. His hat was really big.

"Okay, you guys," Ron said. He picked up a guitar. "One thing we do around the campfire is sing."

Ron strummed his guitar and led the kids in a round of "Home on the Range."

"Are there any requests?" Linda asked when the song was over.

Iris raised her hand. "Do you know 'Dance Like Crazy' by the Jumping Beans?"

Josh rolled his eyes. "That's a rock song. You don't sing that on a ranch."

"What *do* you sing?" Iris asked.

"Glad you asked," Josh said. He stood up and pulled out a harmonica. "I call this little ditty 'Rope Them Dogies.'"

Josh tooted his harmonica. Then he sang to the tune of "She'll Be Comin'

Round the Mountain": "She'll be ropin' them ol' dogies when she comes! She'll be ropin' them ol' dogies when she comes—"

When Josh stopped singing, Bess took her fingers out of her ears. Nancy forced herself to clap.

"Wait! Wait!" Josh said. "There's still the big finish!"

Josh grabbed his lasso and twirled it around his leg. He lost his balance and fell to the ground with a thud.

"Nice try, Tex," Ron said.

Josh mumbled something and crossed his legs.

"Are we just going to sing tonight?" Peter asked Ron and Linda.

"Don't you like to sing, Peter?" Linda asked.

"Sure," Peter said. "But it's hard to sing with marshmallows in your mouth."

"I have an idea," Ron said. "Why doesn't Annie tell one of her famous ghost stories?"

"Yay, Annie!" Linda cheered.

Nancy looked at Annie. She couldn't tell whether she was blushing or glowing from the campfire.

"Okay, okay," Annie said, standing up. "Tonight I'll tell you the story of the drinking horse of Galloping Grits."

Everyone became silent. The only sound was the crackle of the campfire.

Annie's eyes were on Nancy as she began to speak. "Every summer one pony on this ranch . . . disappears."

"Oh, no!" Bess gasped.

Annie nodded. "It happens when the pony wanders out of the stable at night to drink from the lake."

"How do you know they disappear?" Nancy asked. "Maybe they just get lost."

"How do I know?" Annie asked. "Um . . . because they always leave one horseshoe by the lake."

"Wow!" everyone gasped.

"And," Annie went on, "it always happens on the night of a full moon."

"There's a full moon tonight!" George

declared. "I believe that story. Do you, Nancy?"

Nancy shook her head. "It's a good story. But ponies can't just disappear."

Bess gave a little shiver. "I sure hope not," she said softly.

"Buttermilk pancakes, mmmm!" George said at breakfast the next morning. "I'm so hungry I could eat a horse!"

"George!" Bess complained. "Don't say that on a ranch."

"You girls *should* eat a good breakfast today," Mr. Marvin said as he finished his bacon and eggs. "You'll need lots of energy for that trail ride."

Nancy couldn't wait for the trail ride. And she couldn't wait to ride Star.

After breakfast the girls ran to the stable. Nancy looked into Star's stall. She frowned when she saw it was empty.

They ran outside to check the corral. Other ponies were there, but not Star.

Nancy, Bess, and George looked almost everywhere on the ranch. They even peeked inside the barn. They saw lots of chickens, but no Star.

"Hey, Nancy," George said slowly. "Wasn't there a full moon last night?"

"Yes," Nancy said. "So?"

George's dark eyes flashed. "So maybe Star . . . disappeared!"

3

Hot on the Trail

Star disappeared?" Nancy repeated.

"It's possible," George said. "Annie said that every year one horse disappears from the ranch. So why not Star?"

"Quit it, George," Bess begged. "You know how much I hate scary stories."

"Someone here will know where Star is," Nancy said. "You'll see."

Nancy saw Slim walking by.

"Are you girls all set for the trail ride today?" Slim called over.

"Not really," Nancy answered. "I'd like to ride Star, but he isn't around. Do you know where he is?"

"Star?" Slim asked. He gave a little jump. "Gosh! Did you hear that?"

"What?" Nancy asked, wrinkling her nose. She didn't hear anything.

"Coyotes!" Slim cried. "I'd better make sure the chicken coop is locked."

"Did he see Star or didn't he?" George asked as Slim ran to the barn.

"I don't know," Nancy said. "Let's ask Annie. Star is her favorite horse."

The girls ran back to the stable. They didn't see Annie, but they did see Linda and Ron saddling up the ponies.

"There you are," Linda said with a smile. "The trail ride starts soon."

"Linda?" Nancy asked. "Did you see Star anywhere?"

"We looked everywhere and couldn't find him," Bess explained.

Ron and Linda glanced at each other. Then they both grinned.

"Maybe Star disappeared," Ron said with a little laugh.

"Under the full moon," Linda added.

"See?" George whispered to Nancy. "I told you."

23

Nancy stared at Star's empty stall. She *had* to find out where he was.

"Let's round up the ponies for the trail ride," Ron said. He turned to Nancy. "Which one would you like to ride today?"

Nancy's heart sank. She really wanted to ride Star. But she pointed to a speckled pony in the stall next to Star's.

"That's Freckles," Ron said.

While the wranglers saddled up the ponies, Bess turned to Nancy.

"This is starting to sound like a mystery," Bess said in a hushed voice.

"It *is* a mystery," Nancy said. She patted her notebook in the pocket of her overalls. "And I'm going to solve it."

George pumped her fist in the air. "Yes! Nancy Drew—dude ranch detective!"

"Shh," Nancy said. "I don't want the others to know. At least not yet."

The other kids showed up for the trail ride. They were Iris and Peter and ten-year-old twins Nicole and Nicholas.

"Howdy!" Josh said. He walked into the stable with his hands in his pockets.

"Well, howdy, Tex!" Linda said. "Are you fixin' to join us today?"

"You mean . . . ride a horse?" Josh asked with a gulp. "Er . . . not today, ma'am. I've got to go and slop the hogs."

Everyone giggled as Josh ran away.

"I think he's scared of horses." Bess sighed. "Some cowboy!"

Ron and Linda led the ponies out of the stable. The ponies stood in a line as the kids mounted.

"Hi, Freckles," Nancy said when she was in the saddle. "It's not that I don't like you, it's just that I'm worried about Star."

When all the kids were on their ponies, Linda mounted her horse, Lulu. Ron climbed up on his horse, Blizzard.

Then Linda led the line of ponies into the woods. The leaves and twigs on the ground crunched as they rode along the trail. Sunlight peeked through the trees.

The twins rode behind Linda. Then came Peter, Iris, George, Nancy, and Bess. Ron was the last on the line.

I'll write Daddy and Hannah a new

letter, Nancy thought as she rode through the woods. But this time I'll tell them that mysteries can happen *anywhere*— even on vacation.

After riding for half an hour, Linda called for a rest. Everyone dismounted and hitched their ponies to a fence. While the kids sat on the grass, drinking lemonade, Nancy waved her friends over to a big leafy tree. They sat underneath and got to work.

Nancy opened her notebook and wrote "Where's Star?" at the top. A few lines down she wrote the word, "Reasons."

"What are some reasons that Star might be missing?" Nancy asked.

"He disappeared." George jabbed her finger on the page. "Write the legend."

Nancy didn't believe the legend, but she wrote it down for George's sake.

"What if Star was *stolen?*" Bess asked with wide blue eyes. "All cowboy movies have horse thieves."

"Star might have been sold, too," Nancy said. "Dixie told me that he was worth a lot of money."

"And Slim acted weird when we asked him about Star," George said. She narrowed her eyes. "Dixie and Slim—partners in crime!"

Nancy wrote Dixie's and Slim's names in her notebook. "They're just suspects for now," she said. "When we get back to the stable I want to look for more clues."

"Nancy, Bess, George!" Ron called over. "It's time to ride back now."

Nancy quickly shut her notebook. "Coming!" she called back.

"What were you writing back there?" Iris asked as they mounted their ponies.

"A crossword puzzle," George said quickly. "We were looking for a three-letter word for—"

"Thief," Bess said. "I mean—leaf!"

The parade of ponies rode through the woods back to the ranch. This time they trotted straight to the stable.

"Don't forget," Ron told the kids as they dismounted. "There's a trail ride and picnic tomorrow morning at eleven."

While Ron and Linda brought the

ponies to their stalls, the girls waited outside the stable door.

"That's funny," Nancy heard Ron say. "There are no carrots left. Let's get some more from the kitchen."

The girls backed against the stable wall as Ron and Linda walked out.

"Alone at last," George said.

"Let's go!" Nancy said.

The girls ran inside. Nancy peeked into Star's stall. She noticed that Star's feed bucket was still full.

"That's a clue," Nancy said. "Star wasn't in his stall all day."

Nancy wrote "Full feed bucket" in her notebook. Suddenly she heard voices outside the stable.

"The ponies must be back from the trail ride, Slim," one voice said.

"It's Dixie and Slim!" George said.

"We have to hide," Nancy said. She saw a ladder that led up to a hayloft. "Up there!" she said.

The girls scurried up the ladder to the hayloft. They lay on their stomachs and peeked over the edge.

"Ouch!" Bess complained. "This hay feels like pins and needles!"

Nancy heard the barn door creak open. Looking down, she saw Dixie and Slim enter the stable.

"A check for fifteen dollars!" Slim said. He waved a small piece of paper in the air. "That's a pretty penny, Dixie."

"Well, shucks, Slim." Dixie laughed. "That horse was one fine critter."

"They sold a *horse!*" George whispered. "Dixie and Slim sold a horse!"

Suddenly Nancy felt a piece of hay stick her leg. "Ouch!" she cried.

George clapped her hand over Nancy's mouth. But it was too late.

"Who's up there?" Slim demanded.

Nancy froze. They were caught—and they were trapped!

4

Follow That Carrot!

Nancy gripped her notebook. What would they do now?

"Cluck, cluck!" George called down.

"Buck, buck!" Bess joined in.

Nancy smiled. Bess and George were pretending to be chickens!

"Cluck, cluck!" George cried louder. But when she flapped her elbows she knocked Nancy's notebook out of her hands.

"Oh, no!" Nancy gasped.

The notebook hit the ground with a clunk. Nancy peeked over the edge and watched as Dixie picked it up.

"Well, now!" Dixie said. "I didn't know chickens kept diaries."

Bess stuck her head up. "It's not a diary!" she called down. "It's Nancy's blue detective notebook!"

"Bess!" Nancy complained.

"Well, it is." Bess shrugged.

"Busted!" George groaned.

The girls climbed down from the loft.

"So you're a detective, huh?" Dixie asked Nancy. She handed her the notebook.

Nancy nodded. "We heard you say that you sold a horse for fifteen dollars."

Dixie and Slim looked at each other. Then they burst out laughing.

"That horse we were talking about was a *wooden* critter," Dixie explained.

"Wooden?" Nancy repeated.

"The pretty blue horse you liked in the gift shop," Slim said. "A guest bought him this morning."

Slim held out the paper. "See?"

Nancy looked at the paper. It was a check for fifteen dollars. And it had been written by Mr. Marvin.

"Bess," Nancy said. "Your dad bought you the little blue horse."

"Cool!" Bess said.

"That explains *that* horse," George said. "But where's Star?"

Dixie and Slim looked at each other again. This time they weren't smiling.

"Star, huh?" Dixie said slowly.

Slim put his hand to his ear. "Did you hear that?"

"Now what?" George muttered.

"There's a storm brewing," Slim said. "We'd better board up the cowshed, Dixie."

The girls followed Dixie and Slim out of the stable. They stood and watched as the couple ran to the barn.

"What storm?" George asked, glancing at the sky. "It's totally sunny today."

"Oh, well," Nancy said. "*Someone* at this ranch must know where Star is. But I don't think it's Dixie or Slim."

After Nancy crossed their names out of her notebook, she felt Bess tug her arm.

"Here come my mom and dad," Bess said. "They're dressed like cowboys!"

33

Mr. and Mrs. Marvin walked over. They were wearing western-style shirts and white cowboy hats.

"We just got back from the grown-ups' trail ride," Mrs. Marvin said.

"All that riding gave us an appetite," Mr. Marvin said. "How about some lunch in the dining hall?"

"Are you going to eat some more of that red-hot chili, Daddy?" Bess asked.

Mrs. Marvin gave her husband a look of warning. "I think we'll all have sandwiches today," she said.

The girls followed the Marvins toward the dining hall. Suddenly Nancy stepped on something that made a crunch. She looked down and saw two carrots on the ground.

"Carrots!" Nancy said.

"You want *carrots* for lunch?" George asked, wrinkling her nose.

"No," Nancy said. She kneeled down and pointed to two carrots on the ground. "It looks as if someone *dropped* carrots."

"There are some more," Bess said, run-

ning ahead. She picked up three carrots from the ground.

"There's a whole *trail* of carrots," Nancy pointed out. "And they lead right to Josh's trailer."

Bess told her parents they would catch up with them in the dining hall. Then the girls walked quickly to Josh's trailer. As they got nearer, Nancy heard a strange sound coming from inside. Sort of like a loud thump! thump! thump!

George covered her ears. "It sounds like a team of horses in there," she said.

"Horses?" Nancy repeated. She stared at the carrots in her hand. "Horses eat carrots. And Josh's parents were going to bring home a pony."

THUMP! THUMP! THUMP!

Nancy pressed her ear to the trailer door. She heard the sound of Josh's voice.

"Whoa, boy!" Josh was saying. "Whoaaa!"

Nancy's eyes opened wide. "Bess, George," she said. "Could Josh be hiding Star inside this trailer?"

5

Wild West Pest

This trailer is big enough for a horse," Bess said. "Especially a pony."

Nancy knocked on the trailer door. "Josh?" she called. "Are you in there?"

George banged on the door harder.

"We know you've got a horse in there," she shouted. "Come out and give yourself up!"

Nancy rolled her eyes. George was watching too many detective shows on TV.

"We're going in," George decided. She yanked the door open, and the girls dashed inside.

Nancy looked around. She didn't see a pony, just Josh standing in the middle of the trailer and staring at them.

"Well?" Nancy asked Josh. "Where is he? Where is—"

Something furry jumped into Nancy's arms. She began to scream.

"It's a rabbit!" George cried.

"A *gigantic* rabbit!" Bess shrieked.

The rabbit wriggled against Nancy's chest and shoulders. Then it jumped away.

"Get him!" Josh shouted as the rabbit hopped all over the trailer. It jumped across the table and kicked over a bowl of fruit. Then the rabbit jumped on a shelf and knocked books and games to the floor.

"He's out of control!" George cried.

Josh grabbed his lasso and twirled it over his head. "Rope them bunnies!" he shouted. "Yee-haaaa!"

"No!" Nancy shouted. She grabbed Josh's arm and the rabbit bounded out the open door. Everyone was silent as they stared out of the trailer.

"He sounded like a horse," George said with a shrug.

Josh whirled around. He looked mad.

"See what you went and did?" he cried. "You scared away my jackrabbit."

"*Your* rabbit?" Nancy asked.

"Since when?" George demanded.

"When I asked my folks for a pony, they said no," Josh explained. "They said our apartment was too small and I'm too scared of horses anyway."

"We knew that," Bess said.

Josh blushed but went on. "While my parents were on a hike I saw the rabbit sitting in front of our trailer."

"And you brought him inside?" Nancy asked, her eyes wide.

"Sure," Josh said. He pointed to a pile of carrots on the kitchen counter. "I took those out of the stable while you were on your trail ride. You don't think *I'd* eat all those carrots, do you? Gross!"

Nancy folded her arms across her chest. "It's not fair to take an animal out of the wild," she said. "And it's not safe either."

"You should know better than that," Bess told Josh.

"I know *now*," Josh said. He looked at the girls and began to laugh. "Did you really think I had a horse in here?"

Nancy nodded. "A pony named Star is missing. Do you know where he is?"

"How should I know?" Josh asked. He glanced at the window and a smile spread across his face. "Hey! I reckon I found another critter to take back home."

"What?" Nancy asked.

Josh pulled a small red reptile from the windowsill. He held it by its long, wiggly tail. "A lizard!" he declared.

Bess let out a huge scream. She turned around and ran out of the trailer.

"Bess, wait!" Nancy called as she and George ran after her.

"It was just a salamander!" George shouted. "A tiny little salamander!"

Bess whirled around. "I don't care!" she cried. "It was still icky!"

Nancy could see that Bess was very upset. Her eyes were filling with tears.

"All I wanted to do was ride ponies," Bess said. "Now the ponies are disappearing and the place is full of creepy crawlies. I want to go home!"

Nancy patted Bess's shoulder. "You'll feel much better after you eat lunch."

"Yeah," George said. "Maybe they'll have ice cream for dessert."

"Strawberry?" Bess sniffed.

"Probably," Nancy said.

"I feel better already," Bess said with a smile. "Come on. Let's eat."

The girls ate hamburgers and grilled cheese sandwiches for lunch. There was ice cream for dessert—chocolate, vanilla, *and* strawberry.

After lunch the Marvins took the girls to the lake. Mr. and Mrs. Marvin rented fishing poles. The girls borrowed three plastic pails to fish for minnows.

"These minnows are so small they're practically invisible," George said. She skimmed her pail in the shallow water.

Nancy's eyes were on the water, but her mind was still on Star.

"Josh didn't hide Star," Nancy said.

She dragged her pail in the water. "So now we have no suspects. Zero. Zip. Zilch."

"Nuh-*uh*," George disagreed.

"What do you mean?" Nancy asked.

"You're forgetting about the legend," George said. "Star could have disappeared by the light of the full moon. Remember?"

"I remember." Nancy sighed.

The girls continued to scoop up minnows and spill them back into the lake.

"Wow!" Bess said as she lifted her pail. "Wait until you see what I found!"

"A big fish?" Nancy asked.

"No, a big *shoe*," Bess said. "A *really* big shoe!"

"Big deal," George said. "People are always losing their swim shoes."

Bess reached into her pail. She pulled out something silver. "Do *horses* go swimming?" she asked.

Nancy stared at the curved object in Bess's hand.

"It's a horseshoe!" she gasped.

6

Hoedown Lowdown

Do you know what that horseshoe means?" George exclaimed. She dropped her pail on the ground. "The legend is true. Star disappeared and left behind his shoe."

"Like Cinderella," Bess said in a hushed voice. "Except Cinderella didn't disappear."

Nancy didn't want to believe Annie's story. But with Star missing and the horseshoe by the lake—who knew?

"Annie was the one who told us the story," Nancy said. "We have to find her and show her this horseshoe."

The Marvins gave the girls permission to leave the lake. Bess carried the horseshoe in her pail as they ran away from the lake and toward the stable.

"Nancy! Bess! George!" a voice called. "Wait up!"

Nancy spun around and saw Iris.

"Come on, you guys," Iris said. "I need all of you for this way cool game."

"Sorry, Iris," Nancy said. "We don't have time for a game now."

Iris's shoulders drooped. "But I need three more kids to make up a team."

"We can't, Iris," George declared. "Something really important just came up."

"Well, the horseshoe game is important, too," Iris insisted.

Nancy stared at Iris. "Horseshoe game?"

Iris waved her hand. "Come on. I'll show you," she said.

The girls followed Iris behind the dining hall. A bunch of kids were tossing big silver horseshoes across a sandpit. Some of the horseshoes landed over a big spike at the end of the pit.

45

"You get points if your horseshoe lands over the spike," Iris explained.

Nancy looked at the horseshoes lying in the sandpit. They looked *exactly* like the one in Bess's pail.

A boy with curly hair tossed a horseshoe over the spike. "I got one!" he shouted. He jumped up and down. "I'm a lean, mean horseshoe-hurling machine!"

"Show-off," Iris grumbled.

A teenager with a Galloping Grits Staff T-shirt walked over. "My name's Daryl. How would you girls like to toss some horseshoes?"

Bess pulled the horseshoe from her pail. "You mean like this one?"

Daryl's eyes lit up.

"Hey! That must be the one I lost down at the lake," he said. "Sometimes the horseshoes get muddy so I take them to the water to wash them off."

The girls were silent.

"Well, there goes the legend," George finally said with a sigh.

And there goes my last clue, Nancy thought.

* * *

"Why do they call it a square dance when everyone dances in a circle?" George asked that night.

It was eight o'clock. The Galloping Grits Ranch was having a big square dance outside the barn. There were colorful lights hanging from the trees and long tables filled with snacks.

"I'm glad I wore my horseshoe earrings," Bess said, flipping back her hair. "They're perfect for tonight."

Nancy saw Dixie and Slim standing on a small wooden stage. Slim played a fiddle while Dixie sang, "Swing your partner to the right. Then stamp your feet with all your might!"

Nancy giggled. Most of the dancers were bumping into one another, but they looked as if they were having fun.

Josh walked over. He was wearing his rhinestone outfit again. "Do you ladies know how to do the Cotton-Eyed Joe?" he asked.

"What's that?" Nancy asked.

47

Josh rolled his eyes. "It's a dance," he said. "Hel-*lo?*"

"Good-*bye!*" George snapped.

Josh walked away, and the girls decided to snack on barbecue potato chips. Nancy saw Annie at the end of the table. She was pouring ice into the fruit-punch bowl.

"Hi, Annie," Nancy said, smiling. "Do you know how to do those dances?"

"Some of them," Annie said. She crumpled the plastic ice bag. "Oh, well, I've got to go now. See you."

"Wait!" Nancy said quickly. "I want to ask you about Star."

But Annie was too fast. She slipped into the crowd and disappeared.

"Phooey!" Nancy said. "I should have asked her about Star right away."

"We'll probably see her later, Nancy," Bess said. "Now, who wants punch? It's probably nice and cold."

Bess walked to the punch bowl. But instead of grabbing a cup she grabbed her earlobe. "Oh, no!" she cried. "One of my horseshoe earrings just fell off. I think it slipped under the table."

"Let's crawl under the table and look for it," Nancy suggested.

"You mean with my new outfit?" Bess cried. She patted her flowered blouse over her pink shorts. "In all that dirt?"

"Oh, stop being so prissy," George told her cousin.

"That's easy for you to say," Bess said as they crawled under the table. "You're just wearing a grubby sweatshirt and jeans."

Nancy was about to search for the earring when two pairs of feet dressed in cowboy boots appeared behind the tablecloth. Two men were standing right next to the table.

"It was mighty fine of you to invite me to the hoedown, Ron," one man said.

"Ron's out there," Bess whispered. "He has no clue that we're under here."

"Let's just wait a few seconds," Nancy said. "Then we'll surprise them."

The girls were silent as Ron continued to speak.

"Wait until you see Star tomorrow, Wally," Ron said. "I spent all day grooming him."

George bumped her head under the table. Bess grabbed Nancy's arm.

Nancy couldn't believe her ears either. Star was on the ranch, and Ron knew where. The surprise was on *them*.

7

Pony Tail

Nancy!" Bess whispered. "Did you just hear—"

Nancy placed a finger to her lips. She strained her ears to hear more.

"But remember, Wally," Ron said in a low voice. "Don't tell anyone about Star. It's supposed to be a secret."

Nancy held her breath as the cowboy boots walked away. She liked Ron and never thought he would be a suspect.

"Who's this Wally guy?" George asked.

"I don't know," Nancy said. "But let's follow them."

"But you said you'd help me find my earring," Bess said. "You promised."

George heaved a big sigh, but Nancy agreed. A promise was a promise.

The girls searched under the table until Nancy found the earring. When they slipped out from under the table Ron and Wally were already gone.

"We lost him," Nancy said. She stopped in front of the barn and opened her notebook. Then she wrote:

> Ron—knows where Star is.
> Big secret!

"I wonder what the big secret is," Bess said.

"The most important thing is that Star is on the ranch," Nancy pointed out.

"But where?" George cried. "We looked all over!"

Nancy shook her head. She leaned against the barn and felt something behind her back. Turning around, she saw that it was a map of the Galloping Grits Ranch.

"Maybe we didn't look *everywhere,*" Nancy said slowly.

The map was covered with a sheet of clear plastic. The trails were marked with arrows. There were squares for the buildings and a big circle for the corral.

Nancy noticed another circle. But it was near the top and too high to see.

"I wish I were taller," Nancy complained as she jumped on her tiptoes.

"Try this," George said. She grabbed a bucket and flipped it upside down. Nancy hopped on top. Now she could see the circle perfectly.

"It says Cowpoke Corral," Nancy read out loud.

"Another corral?" George asked. "How come we never saw it?"

Nancy saw a line of arrows underneath the circle. "The Cowpoke Corral is at the end of a long trail," she said. "It's called Twisty Trail."

"Wow!" Bess gasped. "Maybe Star's been in that corral all the time."

Nancy jumped down and opened her notebook. She drew a circle for the corral and a squiggly line for Twisty Trail.

"We have to check out the Cowpoke Corral," Nancy said.

"But it looks so far away," George said. "How do we—"

"Hey, you guys," Iris interrupted.

Nancy looked up. She saw Iris and Peter running over. She quickly closed her notebook and slipped it into her pocket.

"Don't be party poopers," Iris joked. She kicked her heels. "Come and dance!"

"It's not hard," Peter said. "It's like the hokeypokey with cowboy hats."

"We'd better join them," Nancy whispered to Bess and George.

Nancy, Bess, and George followed their new friends to the dance floor.

"This is fun," Iris said. "But I can't wait until the trail ride tomorrow."

"It's going to be huge," Peter said excitedly. "Linda just told us we're riding all the way up Twisty Trail!"

The girls stared at one another.

"So?" Iris asked. "Are you going on the trail ride?"

Nancy gave Iris a big smile. "We are now!"

The next morning after breakfast the girls ran straight to the stable. Linda was alone, saddling up the ponies.

"Ron won't be joining us today," Linda said. "He has some work to do."

"I'll bet he does," George muttered.

The other kids showed up for the ride. Iris and Peter were there. So were the twins, Nicholas and Nicole. Nancy was surprised to see Josh.

"We thought you were scared of horses," George said.

"Who, me?" Josh laughed. "Tex Fleckner rides high in the saddle!"

"Your pony is ready, Tex," Linda said. She led a caramel-colored pony over to Josh. "His name is Chewy."

Josh looked up at the pony and gulped. "Maybe that saddle is a bit *too* high," he said. "Do you have a smaller pony than that?"

"Yeah," Iris joked. "But you have to put a quarter in it first."

Josh turned red. "That's so funny I forgot to laugh!" he snapped.

"Okay, kids," Linda said. "Let's mount our ponies and hit the trail."

Nancy was happy to get Freckles again. When everyone was in the saddle they followed Linda out of the corral and into the woods. Nancy rode right behind Josh. The more they rode, the less nervous Josh seemed to be.

"You're doing great, Josh!" Linda called from the front of the line.

Nancy liked Twisty Trail. It wasn't as twisty as a pretzel, but it had lots of turns. They were on the trail for an hour when Freckles began to snort and bob her head.

"What's the matter, girl?" Nancy asked. Freckles gave a soft whinny and trotted on.

"Okay, gang," Linda called. "Time to hitch up the ponies and break for lunch."

The kids stopped at a small picnic

area surrounded by trees. They tied their ponies to a row of hitching posts.

Nancy saw that Josh didn't look nervous anymore. His face was beaming.

"How did you like your first pony ride, Josh?" Nancy asked.

"Chewy is okay," Josh said. "But I think I'm ready for a real horse. You can't lead a cattle drive on a pony."

"A cattle drive?" Nicolas cried. "Give me a break!"

Linda unpacked peanut butter sandwiches and two thermoses of juice.

"Are we riding to the end of the trail, Linda?" Nancy asked as she sipped a cup of apple juice.

"This *is* the end of the Twisty Trail," Linda said.

"It is?" George said. "I mean, time sure flies when you're having fun."

Nancy pulled Bess and George to the side. "The Cowpoke Corral can't be too far from here," she said.

George looked around. "I'll bet it's somewhere behind these trees," she said.

58

"But how do we look for the corral without Linda knowing?" Bess asked.

Nancy thought for a moment. Then she had an idea. She walked back to Linda. "I think we drank too much juice, Linda," she said. "If you know what I mean."

Linda chuckled. "There's no girls' room around here, but there are plenty of bushes. If you know what I mean."

"Bushes?" Bess cried. "Gross!"

"Thanks, Linda," Nancy said quickly. "We'll be right back."

The girls scooted through the trees. Then Nancy saw it—the Cowpoke Corral.

"There it is!" Nancy said.

The corral stood in a field in the distance. Ron and another man were leaning against the fence and talking. Next to them was a trailer hitched to a car.

"There's Ron," George said. "I wonder if Star is in the corral."

Nancy looked closer. The only horse she could see was Ron's horse, Blizzard.

"We have to get closer," Nancy said.

"What if they see us?" Bess asked.

"We'll tell them we're playing hide-and-seek," George said. "Let's go!"

Nancy made sure the men weren't looking. Then she and her friends walked quickly across the field.

They hid behind a haystack near the corral. Nancy peeked around the square bales of hay and listened.

"This pony will be the star of your show tonight, Wally," Ron said.

So that's Wally, Nancy thought.

"Thanks to you, Ron," Wally said. He smiled and shook Ron's hand.

Nancy watched as Wally climbed into his car. As he drove off Nancy could read the words on the side of the trailer: Wally's Wild West Show.

But then Nancy saw something else. Swinging from the back of the trailer was a black tail with silver streaks.

"There's only one horse I know with a tail like that," Nancy told Bess and George. "And it's *Star!*"

8
Shining Star

"So that's it!" George said angrily. "Ron sold Star to Wally's Wild West Show!"

"Star was good enough to be in a show," Bess said. "Everyone knew that."

Nancy leaned against the haystack. She remembered how excited Freckles had been as they neared the end of the trail. She must have sensed that Star was nearby.

"We have to tell Dixie and Slim as soon as we get back," George said.

"Hold your horses!" Nancy said. "We only saw the pony's tail. That's still not enough proof."

"Then what do we do now?" Bess asked.

Nancy knew there was only one thing left to do.

"We have to go to Wally's Wild West Show tonight," Nancy answered.

"No problem." Bess smiled. "My parents love those kind of shows—and the cotton candy!"

The girls waited until Ron was busy riding Blizzard around the corral. Then they hurried back to the woods.

"We're ready to ride back now," Linda told the kids. She looked at Josh. "Think you can handle it, Tex?"

"Are you kidding?" Josh asked. He gave his pony a pat. "Chewy and I are ready for the high-jump!"

The kids sang songs on their way back down the trail. But Nancy had another song on her mind: Twinkle, twinkle, little Star, how I wonder *where* you are!

"George!" Nancy said that night at Wally's Wild West Show. "Your cowboy hat is in my face again."

"Sorry," George said. She was wearing a gigantic green cowboy hat made out of foam rubber. The brim flopped over her face as she ate a corn dog on a stick.

Nancy hadn't bought a rubber hat. She'd bought a flashlight shaped like a cactus. Bess had bought barbecue-flavored popcorn.

Mr. and Mrs. Marvin were sitting right behind them. They were sharing a stick of pink-and-blue cotton candy.

Nancy looked around the tent. Rows of bleachers were filled with people. There was a big riding ring in the middle of the tent. Teenagers wearing cowboy hats walked up and down the aisles, selling programs.

Just then Nancy saw Dixie and Slim sitting on the opposite side of the tent.

"There's Dixie and Slim!" Nancy said.

"Where?" George asked. Her big hat flopped as she spun around.

"Over there," Nancy said.

"Where?" George asked again.

"George," Bess said with a sigh. "You're never going to see a thing with that hat on."

"Okay," George said. She took off the hat. "I'll just wave it in the air."

Music filled the tent as a spotlight hit the ring. The show was about to begin.

First Wally came out and told some jokes. "What do you call a fake horse?" he asked the audience. After a few seconds he winked. "A phony baloney pony!"

"That's cornier than my corn dog," George mumbled.

The first act was a cowboy named Bronco Barry riding a bucking stallion. The audience gasped as the horse almost tossed Barry off his back.

The next act was a woman twirling two lassos at once. Then some cowboy clowns pretended to be chased by a bull. The bull turned out to be two clowns in a costume!

After a few more acts Nancy glanced at her watch. It was getting late.

Maybe Star isn't here, Nancy thought.

Maybe lots of ponies have black tails with silver streaks.

"Now you see why we call it the *Wild West!*" Wally told the audience. He waved toward the opening of the tent. "Next, please give a hoot and a holler for little Miss Annie and her pony— Star!"

Nancy gasped. Bess's popcorn flew out of the carton as she jumped up. George almost dropped her corn dog in her lap.

"Yahooo!" Dixie hollered from the bleachers. "Show 'em what you got, Annie!"

The audience cheered as Star danced, pranced, and counted to four with his hoof.

"So that's where Star was all this time," Nancy said softly.

"He was with Annie," George said.

"Amazing!" Bess sighed.

During the break the girls got permission to look for Annie. They found her brushing Star inside a small stable.

"How did you like our act?" Annie asked the girls.

"It was great," Nancy said. "But we just have a few questions."

"I was expecting that," Annie said with a smile.

"Why wasn't Star around the ranch for the last few days?" Nancy asked.

"I was planning to ride Star in the Wild West show," Annie explained. "I also wanted Star to have privacy while I trained him. That's why I took him all the way out to the Cowpoke Corral."

"Why didn't you tell us you were riding Star in the show?" George asked.

"I wanted it to be a surprise for the guests," Annie explained. "I also didn't want lots of people watching me before the show. It makes me nervous."

Nancy understood how Annie felt. She didn't always want everyone to know she was solving a mystery.

"Guess what?" Bess asked Annie. "George thought Star had disappeared."

George blushed as Annie laughed.

"I made that whole story up," Annie said. "So you wouldn't wonder where Star really was."

Bess waved her hand. "Oh, I didn't believe it for a minute."

"Yeah, right," George joked.

Ron came into the stable. He was carrying a bouquet of flowers.

"Way to go, cowgirl!" Ron said. He handed Annie the flowers. "This is from the folks at Galloping Grits."

"Thanks," Annie said. She turned to the girls. "Ron helped Star get ready for the show. He also helped me keep my secret."

"I wasn't the only one," Ron said. "Dixie and Slim kept Annie's secret, too."

Nancy looked at Bess and George. So that's why everyone had been acting so strange!

"Does this mean that Star has to stay here?" Nancy asked. "Forever?"

"No," Annie said. "He's coming back to the ranch at the end of the week."

"We'll be there at the end of the week," Nancy said. "Can I ride him then?"

"Why wait?" Annie asked. "You can ride him tonight if you'd like."

"Tonight?" Nancy asked.

"In the grand finale parade," Annie said. "There's plenty of room in the saddle for both of us."

"A parade?" Nancy gasped. She was too excited to say more. So George did it for her. She took off her giant hat, waved it in the air, and shouted, "Yee-haaa!"

The parade started right after the last act. Nancy and Annie rode behind the cowboy clowns and Bronco Barry.

"Isn't this fun?" Annie asked Nancy as they trotted around the tent. The spotlight bounced around the ring, and the music was louder than ever.

"Awesome!" Nancy replied.

She could see Bess and George waving from the bleachers. Dixie was giving her a big thumbs-up sign.

Nancy reached over Annie and patted Star's mane. "He was definitely the star of the show tonight, Annie," she said.

"I know," Annie said. "But I think I'm going to change his name."

"You are?" Nancy asked. "To what?"

"To Superstar!" Annie said over her shoulder. "Remember?"

Nancy smiled. How could she forget?

That night Nancy lay in bed. She hoped she would dream about the parade, but there was something she had to do first. Nancy reached under her pillow for her notebook. Then by the light of the moon shining through the window she began to write:

If there's one thing I learned on this case, it's that anyone can have a secret—even a cowgirl. And everyone needs privacy, at least sometimes.

I also learned that a ranch is a real cool place to be—even though it will be good to be back home.

Case closed.

EASY TO READ—FUN TO SOLVE!

**Meet up with suspense and mystery
in The Hardy Boys® are:**

THE CLUES™
BROTHERS

#1 The Gross Ghost Mystery

#2 The Karate Clue

#3 First Day, Worst Day

#4 Jump Shot Detectives

#5 Dinosaur Disaster

#6 Who Took the Book?

#7 The Abracadabra Case

#8 The Doggone Detectives

**#9 The Pumped-Up
Pizza Problem**

#10 The Walking Snowman

#11 The Monster in the Lake

#12 King for a Day

#13 Pirates Ahoy!

#14 All Eyes on First Prize

#15 Slip, Slide, and Slap Shot

**#16 The Fish-Faced
Mask of Mystery**

#17 The Bike Race Ruckus

2389

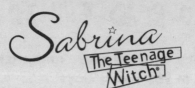

Salem's Tails ®

What's it like to be a powerful warlock,
sentenced to one hundred years in a
cat's body for trying to take over the world?

Ask Salem.

**Read all about Salem's magical
adventures in this series based on the hit
ABC-TV show!**